The Adventures of
Sherrie and Chubbie

Teen Prayer Book

by
**Sherrie
Poitier-Liscombe,
Ph.D.**

Illustration by
Ralston Bailey

The Adventures of Sherrie & Chubbie: Teen Prayer Book
Copyright © 2019 by Dr. Sherrie Poitier-Liscombe

ISBN 978-0-5785-681-6-4
Printed in the United States of America

The Adventures
of
Sherrie & Chubbie Teen Prayer Book

TABLE OF CONTENTS
WHERE CAN I FIND...

Introduction

Prayer is the answer to every situation. It is the means of solving all that ails (hurts/disturbs). It calms and empowers, strengthens, provides focus, cleanses, and gives us all the connection we need to the "Father" to change our lives. Prayer is a direct line to God, and when used appropriately, it invokes our authority and God's hand in our existence. Prayer warriors are strategically placed in the lives of believers and non-believers. They are the protection created by God. They rally the troops, stand in the gap, sound the alarm, and speak power into the lives of God's people. Prayer warriors wage war with the enemy on behalf of God's creation through the power of Christ and the unction of the Holy Spirit. Through their prayer, they beseech God's will, extend His hand, and speak to this world on behalf of Heaven. Sherrie uses her connection with God to empower and encourage her friends, and those she meets because that is what God created her to do. Her purpose entails speaking to God, standing in the gap for her friends, and using her gift to open the eyes and ears of those around her to God and His word. This prayer book will strengthen your connection with God. It takes issues you deal with daily as teenagers and gives you social, emotional, and spiritual guidance as well as scriptures, and prayers you can repeat, add to, or modify (change) to build your relationship with God. Knowing God's word will fuel your ability to communicate with Him and to live a more surrendered and productive life. These perilous times call for a deeper commitment and association. It also affords you an opportunity to see into the prayer life of a prayer warrior, so everyone can pray God's word, connect with God, and be confident that they are not praying amiss (in vain). There are thirty-one prayers; one for each day of the month. There is also a bonus, Thank You prayer for when all you want to do is thank God for what He has already done. The book is designed to guide your prayers as you begin your prayer life, as prayers offer a way for your heart to join with God. Sometimes you may feel you do not know what to say or how to approach God, so these prayers provide insight on getting God's attention. God desires a relationship with each of us and prayer is the "vehicle" we utilize to communicate our hearts to the Father. Though He can read our heart without prayer, He desires us to choose to bond with Him, as that is the only way Love is genuine.

The Adventures of Sherrie & Chubbie Teen Prayer Book is an opening to attach ourselves to our God and as a result, live a fulfilled life.

Let us start with Day One...

Day 1: Relationships

There are different types of relationships: family, professional, hierarchical, friendship, social, adversarial, competitive, and so many more. In these relationships, we must give and take. A relationship must be undergirded (founded on) by mutual benefit for it to be functional. In order to maintain an operational and positive relationship, we must love and allow ourselves to be loved.

The first relationship you must create and sustain is the one you have with God. In doing this, you will learn to have fruitful relationships with others, which is God's will for our lives. It is through these relationships that we lift God to draw men to Him. These relationships are how we share God's word, His love, and our gifts. Relationships are our protection from the enemy as it is in the connection of our lives with God and others which gives us the courage to fight, to stand, to love, and to walk in His will. God pours into us for us to pour into His creation. There are people who will only know God because of their relationship with others. Our representation of our Father beams through everything we are and have, if we are connected to Him. In our relationship with God, we realize the level of love God has for us and this empowers us to endure. God's ultimate desire is to demonstrate unconditional love through us and our lives. This is accomplished through relations with others. We are created to relate, and God ensured this through the diversity of gifts ... all so we would depend on each other!

Scriptures:

A. I Samuel 20:4

B. Numbers 36:9

C. Joshua 13:14

D. Psalms 25:14

E. James 4:4

Dear Father,

Today I come before you to render (give) my heart. You are a loving provider. You are my only true love. As I think of all You are to me, I must say I am nothing without you. I realize I am a sinner who has fallen short (personalize your sin, for example: lied, cheated, shown wrath, taking things without permission), but today I ask You for forgiveness. You are a merciful God, and Your desire is to free my soul. Look upon what I have done and wash me, clean Lord. I thank You for a chance to feel your presence and feel anew. I thank You for a chance to start over daily.

I am grateful that You do not allow my mistakes to ruin our relationship or remove Your plan from my life. Because You love me, You look upon me with mercy, You constantly give me hope, I surrender my life to You. God, I ask You to touch the relationships in my life, starting with our relationship. Open my eyes to Your magnificent love so I can show my appreciation for You and bond with You. As our relationship grows, allow it to rain on my other relationships. May I show Your heart (list relationships with people in your life- even ones that need help ... example: rain love and positivity on my relationship with my mother). God, You allowed people in my life for a purpose. Everything is about purpose in order to fulfill my purpose-I must foster good relationships with people. Help me establish, maintain, and be a blessing in the relationships in my life. May I always approach the relationships with sincerity and as a beacon of Your love. Protect me from negative relationships that would distract me from my purpose and allow me to love and interact without fear, selfishness, doubt, or anger. Father, You are my only hope at influencing others, for Your glory empowers me to be the light You created me to be. I love You God, and I am grateful to be an extension of You in the world. Use me, Lord. In Jesus' Name ... Amen.

In my journal, I sign each prayer ... Love, "Faith." That is God's Nick Name for me. This is part of our relationship, so ask God what your Nick Name is and sign the prayer.

In Jesus' Name,
Amen ...
Love, "Nick Name"

Notes

Day 2: Purpose

Everyone is created for a purpose. It is your purpose that should drive everything you say and do. God uses you for purpose every day. The sooner you know your purpose, the more God can use you and the more fulfilled you will become. Fulfillment is the secret ingredient in joy. We are most unhappy when we operate outside of purpose-God's will.

The greatest element of purpose is the fact that whatever our purpose, we cannot fail at it. We were created to walk in "a thing," so despite fear, obstacles, and hardships, we are destined to be supernaturally successful at it. The world depends on it. Therefore, it has to work. Once you realize this, you become unstoppable if you pursue your purpose.

How do we know our purpose? The more invested we are in our relationship with God; the more He will open our purpose to us. God must trust you will operate in the bounds He gave you rather than try to manipulate your life and your purpose, so you have to be open to His direction. The more you follow Him, the more He will open doors to walk through and direct you on how to get through the preparation. Your purpose has an expected end as it states in Jeremiah 29:11. It is up to you to walk and war to reach that expected end as God unfolds His will to you.

Scriptures

A. Ecclesiastes 3:1 & 3:17

B. Romans 8:28

C. Proverbs 16:3

D. Proverbs 20:18

E. Ephesians 3:11

Dear Father,

I come before You, admiring Your plans for my life despite my past, my doubt, and my fear. Your limitless wisdom has chosen me. You have seen my beginning, middle, and end and have decided to bless me regardless. You are omnipotent, and I honor You because of Your vision and Your supernatural forethought. I yield my love to You to cleanse. I am selfish, and I do not always seek to help others.

I can worry more about how I would benefit and what I need than others and I ask Your forgiveness (confess your personal sins here and be honest, brutally/honest with God because He already knows). I need You to send my sins to the sea of forgetfulness, so I can begin afresh and anew. I need to feel Your loving arms around my heart, so I can hear directly from You. I thank You for forgiveness; a second, third ... a tenth chance and for the opportunity to shape my heart. I thank You for Your unconditional heart and love for me. I thank You for the confidence to approach You for healing and to find out what You want from my life. I thank You for who You are to me and how You have touched me.

Thank You for being a promise keeper. Today I come before You to seek Your will for my life. You created me in Your image and likeness, so I could touch the hearts and minds of those You place in my life for Your glory. You did this, so I could lift You up to them and You could draw them. It is Your will to fulfill my purpose, so people are saved. Thank You, Lord, that You love us enough to create different people with varied gifts to reach diverse individuals. For my gift of (list those things you do well; things you think about; enjoy or want to do but are afraid to try), as each day is an opportunity to grow in it. Your anointing breaks yokes and empowers me to stand for You. As I walk, continue to pour.

Do not let me go on my own, but fill me with Your word so I can represent You. As I surrender, open me up more. I desire to use every gift in me to impact Your people. As I operate for Your glory to change my life, give me fruit so people can see and bear witness to Your hand in my life. My life is to be used again to draw people. I am so grateful for the answering of my prayer. Thank You for opening my eyes to my purpose and for giving me the desire to seek it. As I earnestly seek, open me more and more.

In Jesus' Name,
Amen ...
Love, "Nick Name"

Notes

Day 3: Depression

When you are "overly" preoccupied with the sadness you feel, you are trapped in depression. People going through the emotions of hurt and pain with no end in sight are experiencing depression. Depression is a state that can sneak up on you and overwhelm you. It begins as a feeling you are justified in experiencing because something sad has occurred. Why did it happen? What could you do to stop it? Why did your family/God allow it? You become locked in your own emotions playing the issue over in your mind endlessly. It is not God's will that we remain "sad." He has created us with joy, peace, and love at our core. It is the cares of this world and our own imaginations, which take us out of His will for our lives and lead us to a path of despair. God's word says, "The steps of a good man are ordered by the Lord: and he delighteth in his way," and "Though he fall, he shall not be utterly cast down, for the Lord upholdeth him with His hand."

Knowing that our lives are ordered by God, we know that if we are experiencing heartache and pain, which take our happiness, we can be sure it is temporary. We have delight and joy in God's way and we work in that way because our steps are directed. That is a promise that we can depend on and look to when we have failed. God is merciful and as we repent, and God forgives us, we renew our relationship with Him; our Creator who directs our path and our heart is restored, lifting depression.

Today, realize that dark times are a part of life, but just as it is sure it will come, the promise that dark times are temporary is just as sure. We must ask God to lift us up to the joy within our relationship with Him.

Scriptures

A. Jeremiah 29:11

B. Hebrews 6:19

C. Romans 12:12

D. Romans 15:13

E. Psalms 42:5

Dear Father,

I come to You with a heavy heart. I cannot see beyond my pain. Day in and day out I feel the agony of my situation. I have tried to face it but seems like it is overtaking me. I know Your word promises me peace and joy, but I cannot find it. I have cried, prayed, worried, and tried to figure out how and why this is happening to me. The more I think on this issue, the deeper I fall into depression. I need to be free ...free to love, free to forgive, and free to just smile again. I want to be free to look at where I am headed. You believe that I have made it, even before I see it. I will not allow this feeling to continue to hold me hostage, when I know I can depend on You. I need You to show me the way out. I trust You want me to know joy. I know Your word promises me that I can look to You for answers. It says You have planned my Life. You have seen me through this point already as my end has already been created. I just need to walk in faith, so I choose You and all You have for me. I choose love. I choose forgiveness. I choose life. Thank You for the privilege to lean on You. Thank You for restoring my heart. Thank You, God, for all You do and are.

In Jesus' Name,
Amen ...
Love, "Nick Name"

Notes

Day 4: Fear

Have you ever been afraid? The kind of afraid where you could not do or say something. You could not finish a task, nor could you move? Fear paralyzes us physically, emotionally, and spiritually if it is not in the right perspective. Luke 12:5 warns to only fear He who hath "power to cast into hell." The enemy must get God's permission to even approach us and, in that permission, he has limits. This allows us to feel safe. Though fear is a natural reaction to the unknown, we do not have to allow it to consume us. That is when we do not trust God. He expects us to be afraid, but He has given us His word to combat those times.

Courage is not the absence of fear, but the heart to face it and the mind to walk through it. If we truly trust God, fear is temporary and passing. We should have a level of fear to keep us safe and ensure we don't do things that could hurt us, but fear should never linger.

The fear of God the Bible talks about is a reverence for His supreme authority and His omnipotence, omnipresence, and omniscience. Basically, this means God is all over the place at the same time, all of the time, and knows everything. Therefore, we cannot run, hide, or trick Him with our warped thoughts, or actions so we should walk in His presence as the Father that He is. Everything we say or do should honor Him and if it does not, we may be subject to judgment.

Yes, He is merciful, and He is patient, but we must live our lives with gratitude, not taking advantage of His love. That is what it means to have a "fear or reverence" of God. Fear is not of God. He tells us to speak boldly, live boldly, and love boldly. God is love and love eliminates fear. Knowing God loves us allows us to walk fearlessly. Live each day proving God's love and you will defeat fear indefinitely. We know that despite what we face, He already prepared a way for us to triumph.

Scriptures

A. Exodus 20:20

B. I John 4:18

C. Proverbs 1:7

D. Psalms 34:9

E. Psalms 2:11

Dear Father,

I come before You today with an expectancy. I expect You to exhibit love. I expect to show You my heart. I expect to live my life in Your will. I desire Lord to live without fear. You are my heart My love is dedicated to revering You and in that I must deny fear. I must find courage in Your word and in my purpose. I know You created me, God, to live victoriously and that comes with walking in purpose despite not knowing. Each day I see Your hand in my life and though I know You are with me I still have moments that I doubt. That doubt builds and becomes fear. I do not want to be afraid, and I won't allow fear to keep me from my relationship with You; touch my destiny.

I ask You to give me hope, instill in me a clean heart to hear from You God so when I feel afraid, I can hear Your voice to combat the fear. Renew in me a right spirit so I can walk in Your will; protecting me from the fiery darts of the enemy. My shield of faith God encourages me to trust and believe. The sword, Your word gives me words to speak to bind fear on the Earth, so it can be bound in heaven.

God, I thank You for the ability to pray and to call on You for protection; for anointing that bans the enemy from my life. Thank You for mercy, grace, love, and the wisdom to seek Your face. As You continue to equip me to live for You God, I will be careful to give You all the honor, praise, and glory. I love You God, and I am grateful for Your agape (unconditional) love.

In Jesus' Name,
Amen ...
Love, "Nick Name"

Notes

Day 5: Anger

"Be ye angry and sin not. Let not the sun go down upon Your wrath." -Ephesians 4:26. Anger is an expression of annoyance I am annoyed; displeasure, I am displeased; or hostility, I am hostile. These emotional responses are usually due to a perceived hurt. When we feel like someone has wronged us, spoken ill of us, or done something offensive, we become angry.

Just like fear, anger is a natural response to things that occur. The Bible even gives us permission to "be," angry, yet it cautions us to sin not. When anger is permitted to remain, it leads to wrath, the sin of taking matters into our own hands. God does not mind us having emotions, but when we act on those emotions we sully (dirty) His name. As Christians, we represent Christ; -Christian is "Christ- like" so if I am angry and I use profane language, I have embarrassed God. I have decided I am the judge and should dispense justice, rather than turning it all over to Him. Anger, when used to fuel passion, is a great tool. It does not allow us to sit back and concede to defeat or injustice. When we sanction (allow) anger to feed our sense of commitment to Christ, we will fight using God's word and spiritual techniques, not our fleshly ideas. Anger can lead you to pray to address your problems. It can guide you to spiritual awakening and your inner strength, but it must be surrendered to God, so He can show you how to deal with it in His manner. If we choose to do it on our own, we risk being turned over to wrath. In a church service, I heard that anger is not our enemy ... it is a hater.

A hater is jealous of our brilliance and wants to take us off our game. An enemy wants to destroy you, so you never reach your purpose, they have more vigor in coming after you to get access to your heart through anger. Wrath is the true enemy, and it uses the hater's anger to gain control of your heart.

Anger deprives you of happiness and joy. It does not allow forgiveness, and it also deprives us of mutual respect. People who confess to having anger issues do so because it is easier to blame the emotion rather than decide to speak to what is causing the emotion. The Bible speaks of anger, and even Jesus was angry when He came into the temple and found people cheating the community in a house that was created to be a resource for the needy. We must stand up to our enemies, but in God's will, way, and word, not our own tactics. Use God's word to speak to your emotions. Anger can be subsided when we place our emotions, feelings, and love in God's hands.

Prayer allows us to be honest with God about our hurts, frustrations, annoyances, displeasure, and hostilities toward others and their actions. If we see the things that happen as actions and not hold grudges toward people who, like us, are not perfect, we can deal more positively with our anger. Use your heart for good and not evil and anger will not be able to reign. We have a right to be angry, but we do not have the right to allow anger to hold us hostage and consume us, so we retaliate.

<u>Scriptures</u>

A. James 1: 19-20

B. Ephesians 4:31

C. Proverbs 19:11

D. Psalms 37:8

E. Proverbs 15:1

Dear Father,

Each day I awake grateful to be alive. I am grateful to have health and strength. I am also grateful for a relationship where I can come to You with my heart open. You know me. You see me. You love me, and I love You too. It is my heart's desire to please You and to walk in greatness for Your glory. I am concerned Lord because I am often angry. Some days the anger is because of people, school, my family, even my friends. I look at the world and I am unhappy with where I fit in, where I stand, and how I am progressing. I do not like how things are going in my life. I feel annoyed with all the expectations of teachers, my family, and people in general. I feel like I am trying to be good enough all the time. Everyone has an opinion on my life, the things I say, things I do, and how I live, and I am tired of it! I do not want to be pressured and pushed to "be successful." My family wants me to do more than they did, How? They only talk to me when they want to complain, and I am sick of all the judgment and constantly trying to fit in at school with different people as if I am not already displeased with myself. Why do others feel the need to comment on my life? That makes me so angry. People feed me false dreams, lie about their commitment to me, how much they like/love me and when I do not respond in the manner they see fit, they act like I am wrong. When do I get to make them feel like they make me feel? If I cannot fight back, when will You put them in their place Lord? I need Jehovah Nissi (My banner-protection). I need You God to stand-up for me. I pour my heart out to You Lord, asking You to defend my heart so I can let this anger go. I no longer want to be angry at so much of my life. I want to turn it over to You completely, but I need help surrendering. I want to follow Your word I want to be a presentation of You and I need to be released from this emotion Lord so it does not control who I am. Thank You, God, for rescuing me from my own emotions. Thank You for understanding my heart. Please cover me with Your love and blood.

In Jesus' Name,
Amen...
Love, "Nick Name"

Notes

Day 6: Doubt

To please God, we must have faith! In Hebrews, we learn that God says pleasing Him is based on our faith. It does not say it will be difficult to please God, but impossible without faith. Trust is non- negotiable. God deserves our complete trust. Everything He does is to bless us, even if we do not agree.

For in Jeremiah 29: 11, God tells us that He knows what plans He has for us to prosper us and not to harm us. If we know that He promises to prosper us, we can use this word to speak in our lives when we face doubt. Doubt shows up when we are not close enough to God to hear clearly. Doubt is a product of our limitations. We feel we are not able to handle something in our life so we doubt our "call" (purpose in God); we can doubt our direction; we may even doubt our salvation. That doubt is seeded in our imperfections, not God's.

It is usually a by-product of failure. If we thought we were supposed to pass a test and we fail, we doubt our abilities, our intelligence, and the efficacy (effectiveness) of our prayer strength. We think that God is not hearing us, that He does not care, or we are not worth Him intervening. Though God tells us He is concerned about what concerns us, we still doubt this if we do not get our way, or God does not go in the direction we are "sure" He should go. Doubt can only be reduced through a closer relationship with God and constant reminders of how He desires to prosper us above all else. Doubt and faith cannot co-exist as long as doubt lives within, we have blocked our faith.

Prayer allows us to confide in God, request His guidance, and hear from Him to build our faith. As faith grows, it destroys doubt. We may never rid ourselves of all doubt, but we should as we grow completely in Christ and our relationship matures, reduce it to undetectable levels. Doubt is the enemy of a mature Christian and should be banished from our lives.

Scriptures

A. John 20:27

B. Matthew 14:31 & 21:21

C. James 1:6

D. Matthew 28:17

E. Mark 11:23

Dear Father,

Thank You for Your love. Thank You for being my hope; my love. Thank You for prospering me and allowing me to have a relationship with You, as I continue to learn about Your will and purpose for my life. I want to draw closer to Your heart. I want to hear from You, feel Your strength holding me up. I want to trust Your promises and take You at Your word. I want to depend on You for every inch of my life. I desire to connect with You on a level that opens every avenue of my life. God, You said You have plans for me and I want to live out those plans. I need to believe You and I will. I will not allow the enemy to distract me with doubt or block my faith. I want to please You and I cannot do it without binding doubt, so I bind it through the blood of Jesus. Your word says what is bound on Earth will be bound in heaven. I loose faith and what is loosed on Earth is loosed in heaven. My heart is open to You God, so You can dwell in me and I in You for Your seeds of faith and Your promise for my Life. As my doubt dwindles, empower my faith to move mountains of fear, pain, inadequacies, lack, and disbelief.

In Jesus' Name,
Amen...
Love, "Nick Name"

Notes

Day 7: Loneliness

When you have the 'depressed' feeling of being alone, loneliness has set in. Loneliness involves solitary time without companions; isolating yourself for negative reasons. People can be in a crowded room and still experience loneliness. It is not about being in the company of people, but being connected to people.

People who experience loneliness will not socialize for fear of being rejected, judged, or ignored. Loneliness creeps into people unnoticed at first and when it has fully set in, it will cause you to make more excuses to continue in the state. Sadly we blame others and explain why it makes sense. We defend ourselves and convince ourselves we are protecting our hearts. The enemy has convinced us we cannot protect ourselves against loneliness. But God is a God of unity and covenant, so loneliness is not of God. God is love and love causes connection.

God sanctified Jesus to connect to us, so we would never concede (give up) to remain in a lonely state. We must decide to relate to others. We must take purposeful steps to commune, worship, and share with our neighbors. Prayer is a connector and discernment, the ability to sense someone else's connection to God, empowers us to bind loneliness. We are friends to God, heir to the throne and through our lineage, we bond and come together for God's glory. We do not have to be lonely because God is omnipresent and through prayer, we have access to Him twenty-four hours a day, seven days a week. When you feel like You have no one on your side, be reminded that God will never leave nor forsake you.

Scriptures

A. Deuteronomy 31:6

B. Romans 8:31-38

C. Psalm 25:26

D. Psalm 68:5-6

E. Psalm 139:7-10

Dear Father,

Thank You for a day to come before You to be blessed. You love me most and best and for that I am grateful. Thank You, God, that I can open my lonely heart to You and be comforted. Thank You for how much You love me; how You sacrificed Your son to reconnect with me. God, I admit I have tried on my own to shake this feeling, but I have been unsuccessful. I have allowed the enemy to isolate me, so I would wallow in the loneliness and miss my call. I desire to be free... free to love and share... free to commune with You, my family, and the world. I desire to move past that attempt to hold me hostage. Lord, I need You to desperately touch my heart and change it. Do not let me pull away. Draw me in, mend my lonely heart, and cause me to live for You and lead people to seek You when they are lonely. I want to be a living testimony that loneliness is not our destiny. In You, I can unite friends, family, and nations. I know You are with me. When You feel distant, I can call on your name and you will be there. You have promised to never leave me. When I crave a physical connection, send me Godly friendships and agape love. Use me and my life as an example of how to overcome.

In Jesus' Name,
Amen ...
Love, "Nick Name"

Notes

Day 8: Weight

Are you skinny enough for yourself, but too "fat" for friends and others? How many people believe you should or "could" lose some weight? Do you feel you should lose some weight? If so, why? Because people say so, health reasons, or just so you can look good in smaller clothes? Do you feel unattractive or you believe you could feel "cuter /fine?" Have people stated they would like you or date you if you were "skinny or skinnier?" Have people told you, you would be cuter if you were skinny? Do you know what you should weigh for your height and build (size)? These questions speak to the heart of how you feel about weight. Many times, our views concerning weight are derived (determined) from what others say to us, how others feel about us, and what comments they will post on social media or speak about our weight. Each one of us must be comfortable in our own skin unless our weight is life-threatening.

Obesity, being extremely overweight, can lead to diabetes, hypertension, and other health ailments. Our bodies are placed under strain if our weight is too far beyond the suggested weight limits. If this is not the case, but you have a few layers here or there that you feel need to go, then there are ways to lose weight. If the pressure to lose weight is from external means such as family, friends, or classmates, you can deal with it through prayer. Weight control is a state of mind that can be managed through commitment. If that commitment is led externally, by others rather than internally, it will cause us to be unsuccessful in our pursuit to lose weight, and this can lead to depression and/or anxiety. Again, this can be avoided with a fervent (powerful & focused) prayer where we can call on God to assure us that He created us and loves us the way we are. Bulimia and Anorexia are due to the state of mind of people. Before you take on the negative view of weight or accept others' opinions of your weight, ask yourself this:

1. **Is this my problem or theirs?**
2. **Is it a health issue?**
3. **Do I truly want to do something about the weight?**
4. **If I don't lose weight, will I be okay mentally?**
5. **What do others have to gain by judging my weight?**

Once you have the answer to these questions remember, prayer is again always the answer.

Scriptures

A. Corinthians 6:19-20

B. Romans 12:1-2

C. I Timothy 4:7-9

D. Romans 8:1-4

E. Isaiah 5:1-2

17

Dear Father,

Thank You for being a God that is concerned about what concerns me. Each day Lord I am battling my physical weight as well as my thoughts about weight. I enjoy eating and having the freedom to have what I like. I know You created us to rule over the land and everything that dwells upon it. In our history man gave up the right to rule and reign to satan. Though satan is the prince of the air, we still have dominion, through our relationship with You. As Your heir we can declare, we can bind, and we can loose because You are the Creator. We and the Earth are Your creation, and through Your redemptive (forgiving) blood, we can regain power and control of this Earth. That is why we can fight weight issues and overcome unhealthy desires to take care of our bodies, so weight is not a problem. If we are too thin or too heavy, it is unhealthy, so today I ask You to be the judge.

Look at my body and my heart and lead me to a healthier way of life. Do not allow me to be obsessed. Cause me to seek You as a light in this area. Do not allow me to be an emotional eater or do unhealthy things because mentally I feel overweight. Provide me with Godly counsel. You are "Jehovah Rapha," my healer, and I depend on You for sound advice. As You care for me Lord, teach me to care for myself and through my good eating habits and control, allow me to be an example for others. As my health prospers, I will be sure to honor You. God, I know my weight demonstrates me treating my body as a temple and though my flesh is not connected to You, it does house Your spirit, so I want to treat it as an honorable dwelling.

I want You to know I am grateful for all You have done; how You have kept me healthy despite my lack of control or respect for keeping my body healthy. I am grateful You are giving me an opportunity to live better and I thank You for loving me enough to assist in weight management. As I work on my health, strengthen and encourage me. Even if You must chastise me to get my attention my desire is to please You and to live long enough to finish the work You have for my life. I rebuke any weight related illnesses, diseases, or curses. I release a healthy flow of blood, insulin, and peace.

Touch my mind to strengthen my will to lose weight and reinforce my resolve. I pray for success and support to help me with this weight journey. Provide me with strong, lasting strategies to keep the weight off. Build my self-esteem as I work towards weight loss and protect my heart, mind, body, and soul against naysayers, haters, and those that would not back me up on the journey. Do not allow their negative words or gestures to penetrate my heart, mind, or psyche (mental thoughts). I can do all things through Christ that strengthens me.

In Jesus' Mighty Name,
Amen...
Love, "Nick Name"

Notes

Day 9: Self-Esteem

Song of Solomon is a love letter written to God. Every day I take time to write to God, to tell Him I love Him, discuss how I feel without holding back, and express how I see things. In Song of Solomon, the author writes, "you are altogether beautiful my love; there is no flaw in you." It discusses God's ultimate beauty. God is our love and He is perfect. God is love, therefore - love is perfect. In love, we live out perfection because it stems from the perfection well, God. Knowing this, we should see ourselves in a positive light. We should see the seed that is planted in us as perfect; a gift of love from the embodiment (source) of love, God. How can we feel "low" about ourselves when:

1. **We are born for purpose!**
2. **We are born with all we need to be successful in our purpose!**
3. **It is God's goal for life to fulfill purpose!**
4. **Fulfilling purpose glorifies God!**
5. **God's glory shines through us and gives us hope to fulfill purpose in people's lives!**
6. **God's anointing draws people!**
7. **Anointing-fulfilled purpose pleases God!**
8. **When God is pleased, it opens more gifts that lead to hope emanating from everything you say and do!**

Positive self-esteem builds as you work out your purpose. Negative self-esteem is the result of the lack of progress with or towards your purpose, ignoring your purpose, or walking in elements that are of your own will. Anything ordained by God will build you up leading to a positive outlook. Don't think there will not be a test, times of darkness or obstacles, but if you remain true to your God-given and directed destiny, God will build you to be unstoppable and that is how positive self- esteem is maintained. Self-esteem should not be a driving force in your life. It is part of your life and can provide- strength or weakness depending upon how it is viewed. If you allow it, it will dictate your emotions, mood, thoughts, actions, and it will control you, but if you allow it to be fed by your accomplishments and victories over obstacles- it will be an element of influence. People who exude a positive self- outlook attract people and empower others to excel. Self-esteem- is controlled by You (self) not vice- versa. Who is in control of your growth? You or your self- esteem?

Scriptures

A. Philippians 4:13

B. Psalms 46:15

C. Proverbs 31:25

D. Ephesians 2:10

E. Psalms 139:14

19

Dear Father,

I thank You for a glorious day. I call it glorious because I have conquered death; I have a relationship with my Creator, and I have a clear mind to pray about my self-esteem. Lord people kill themselves every day because they feel lost, less than human, undeserving of life, or just have low self-esteem. They see themselves differently than You do. You promised us we have a reason to live; You said You created us for Your glory. You designated us to change lives and I am grateful to walk in it daily.

The world, I do not believe you! I don't see what they see; I don't hear broken promises and I can't see my past hurt, anxiety, fear, displeasure, impatience, flaws, or insecurities. I know what You have said Lord about me; I see others disappoint You; I see some negative views, yet I bind negative images, depressing thoughts, as well as word declarations or flaws about me.

I bind it, on Earth so it will be bound in heaven. I lose ideals, perfection, positive views, desires, direction, declaration, and positive results in my life, through the power of Your blood. It is loosed on Earth as it is in heaven. Today I stand on Your words about me. I stand on the knowledge that I am made in Your image, so I am chosen, blessed, and paid for in full. My life is a replica of You; it is bought by Your blood; surrendered to Your will and acceptable to You because of the blood not because of me. You love me unconditionally and because You do, I am wanted. I am Your righteousness, so I will not feel negatively about me. That is in direct violation of what You feel, declared, and promised, so to "not" forgive me is selfish and sinful.

For You have cast out my sins, paid for them in advance, and are asking me to be a light to others. You want to use my life to minister, strengthen, guide, and to share. Despite my needs, fears, inadequacies, You use me as a bridge to connect You with someone who doesn't know You. I am chosen to do this because of love not because of me.

You decided I was enough. You declared I am worthy, and I embrace that today. I answer the call to represent You. I thank You for choosing me and I am grateful for a life of dedicated connection, love, and positive self-esteem. I am grateful to see myself striving and lifting You, so You can draw others. Thank You, God, for Your choice.

In Jesus' Name,
Amen...
Love, "Nick Name"

Notes

Day 10: Jealousy & Envy

There are times when we are unhappy with who we are, what we have, and what we believe others have. There are also times when others feel that way about themselves and us. We look at famous, rich, and successful people, without knowing how they achieved all they have, and we allow envy to creep into our heart, knowingly or unknowingly. Jealousy causes division, fear, and mistrust of people and God. It destroys relationships despite as I said in Day 1, relationships are needed and are how we live and flourish.

I have experienced people who dislike me because I have the gift to draw youth in, love them, inspire them, look past their issues, and because of their love for me I have had people try to undermine (sabotage or mess up) my work and exert (apply) power over me to prove they are better than I am. But I always remind myself that I am God's creation. What God has for me is for me, and who He has created me to be cannot be undone or thwarted (frustrated) by what others think, feel, or try to do to me. I will excel in what He has created me to be because I was created to do it. I am who God called. I am who He is using, I am a great nation, a great representative of my God and His righteousness. I will not let how I feel about people or myself interfere with the call on my life.

To fight jealousy, you must remember God created You to do and be something and someone. If you trust that you are perfect in what He created you to do, there is no need for you to be jealous. No one can do what you were created to do. You are not replaceable, nor can you be substituted. You need God in order to be perfect as He has planted a perfect seed inside of you. Your relationship with God is where perfection will bloom, it is how you win! Winners are not jealous if we love the Lord. The enemy will use people to attack us through envious thoughts and actions. You and your gifts are always a victorious opponent.

The world is full of doubters that will try to convince you, your gift is not as powerful as it really is. Knowing that you will never be rid of these people, you must learn to win the war against them. You must first realize it is not the person, they are being utilized (used) by the enemy to attack God through you. The enemy does not have the strength to fight God directly, so he tries to come after you as God's weakness, yet God protects and lends His spirit and the blood of Jesus to war on your behalf. God's promise is that you have more with you than against you because you have Him! You are blessed and highly favored, therefore, you are in a war that you already have victory over! Through "Jehovah Nissi," your banner; your protection.

Scriptures

A. I Corinthians 13:4

B. Ecclesiastes 4:4

C. James 4:11

D. Proverbs 14:30

E. Philippians 2:3

Dear Father,

I am thanking You for a connection that protects. Because of our relationship, I am gifted and can use my gifts for Your glory. Because that is the end goal, I don't have to be jealous. You created me for a reason and because I can stand tall and I am able to be a blessing to others, I conquer every day. I thank You for covering me and protecting my heart. Thank You that I have true love with You as it wards off jealousy. Thank You for changing my views of what I have and showing me my seed is perfect and through Your spirit empowering me to success, I can operate supernaturally with You and with that I am constantly growing and winning.

I don't have to fight those who are also gifted because I have my own blessings. I don't have to fight those who are jealous of me because You did not gift them in my arena, so they cannot touch me. I am invincible, as long as I remain in my gifted area. I am unique; I am gifted; I am blessed, and I am surrendering myself fully to be in Your service. I am grateful God that I can hold on to You and Your word. I can stand tall in You and Your love. Thank You, God, for opening my heart and soul for me to walk in what you purposed for me. I am honored to be chosen by You, Lord. I admit I doubt sometimes, but I pray for strength and direction. I want to fulfill all you have for me as that is where joy lies. I desire my life to be a witness of Your greatness.

In Jesus' Name,
Amen...
Love, "Nick Name"

Notes

Day 11: Self-Control

"I have no self-control!" This is a popular quote from people today, especially young people. I hear students talk about they cannot sit still, stop talking, or refrain from cursing or being rude and disrespectful. Things that are offensive, like profane language or disrespectful comments, have no limit. The amazing part is that it is called "self" control because that is how it is seen and how it is managed and therefore, how it is named or described. No one has control over another person; people can convince or influence, but the only control is "self" executed.

God does not even exert His will over you... you must choose to follow Him. A parent, guardian, or adult will tell you what to do and give you rewards, or consequences based on your compliance (following directions). The Bible instructs You on how to behave and utilize strategies against the enemy. When the enemy tries to persuade, bully, inflict his will on your life, remember, ultimately it is up to you ... It is "self" directed! We make the decision to follow, go our way, or be obedient. We decide if what we want is worth striving for, resisting, or if what we need to do is doable. If I use profanity non-stop, I am still in control because I decide when to cease (stop). I suffer the consequences of my actions, so I must remember that when I am deciding to behave in a certain way.

Sometimes we have medical issues that influence our behavior, but I control if I take the medication to give me the "mind" to do the right thing. If I have a seizure and cause an accident, that is within my control if I have medical direction and do not follow it.

A person cannot say they do not have "self" control because that is all we do have really, the ability to control our own actions. God created us with "free will" so we could choose to serve Him because we wanted to, not out of obligation. True love is given-surrendered, not required. It is a choice. It is ordained, so you have the ultimate choice, to serve or not. You have God fashioned "self" control.

That being said, you may have a lack of responsibility; a lack of morals; or a lack of "self" worth. When you lack self-worth, you will not do things in your best interest. This is where a lack of "self- control" really fits into the picture. People who claim to lack self-control truly lack self-love or worth. Because God is love. A relationship with Him permits your eyes to be opened to self-love and worth.

You are His perfect creation. He produced you in His image to be His choice, His righteousness, and because of that, there is no mistaking it. It's a relationship. You pray and are empowered to make perfect decisions. When you are connected, that is where the definition of self begins, it enables you to see yourself as an image of God, which is how you were created and how God sees you.

Scriptures

A. Galatians 5:22-23

B. I Corinthians 10:13

C. Proverbs 25:28

D. II Peter 1:5-7

E. I Corinthians 9:24-27

Dear Father,

I thank You for creating me in Your image, so I can represent You. I have self-control because I was shaped to rule and reign, and through good decisions, I exhibit my ability to serve others; to put others first; to walk in Your will and in doing so I demonstrate Your perfection. I reflect You as You dwell in me and I in You; with You as a moral compass, I will always address my life and choices with self-control. My control is fashioned after Your love because I hide Your word in my heart, so I might not sin against You. In that declaration, I make beneficial decisions and live a surrendered, self- controlled life.

You, God, are my only hope in a world that tries to drive me out and tries to exploit my weaknesses from the past. I commune with You in prayer; read Your word, and hear revelation from my pastor and Your spirit. I grow in my ability to control negative actions. I can see Your hand in my life and I follow Your lead. God, you are my moral compass. You, God, keep me grounded and Your word keeps me educated and protected. When I try to listen to myself, my spirit man arises and directs me back to You. I am grateful for that unction (direction).

Thank You, God, for Your sacrifice and creating me in Your own image so I would have a fighting chance to overcome the enemy's tactics and thank You for allowing me to be a model for my family, so they would have a chance. I also thank You for cleaning up my life to follow You and walk in Your way. You, God, have just been so amazing, patient, and the fact that You have built me to live victoriously through informed self-control, demonstrates Your supernatural mercy for me.

In Jesus' Name,
Amen...

Love, "Nick Name"

Notes

Day 12: Honesty

Living life to create a legacy (lasting demonstration of our work) is the goal of a leader and servant. All we do should be in the pursuit to lend our names to leaving a legacy. I read a quote once that honesty is the richest legacy there is.

When people speak about you as a person, a leader, or any title you had, it should have the legacy of honesty and integrity attached. A "good" name is more coveted than money or any other evidence of success. When people can speak of you as one of honesty and integrity, you become worth more than riches. Being honest opens the door to more opportunities, more success, and sometimes more heartache. People don't always appreciate your honesty, but they will love and respect it eventually. Don't be afraid to step out and tell the truth because it will connect you with God and He will protect you if you are honest; in His will. Honesty allows people to refer you to others and allows God to trust you.

Once you have proven your character, God will promote (give you success) you. There will be times when lying will be easier, more acceptable to man, and safer. It will seem that way, but being on the negative (trouble) side of God is far more dangerous than accepting the consequences of man or the enemy when you tell the truth. When you are tempted to lie to get out of trouble, out of a bad situation, or just to get what you wanted accomplished, remember you are denying God's ability to help you out and turning your back on the relationship you share with Him. Lying is never harmless.

Though God forgives and forgets, satan never stops using it against you and it allows him to enter your problem and your life. You must protect your connection with God with the truth, trusting that He sees and hears all and will get you safely to your destination despite your error as this is how you remain victorious. Never tell God He cannot help you by telling a lie. The loss of connection is never worth it.

Scriptures
A. II Corinthians 8:21
B. II Timothy 2:15
C. Ephesians 4:25
D. I Peter 3:10-12
E. Proverbs 12:17 & 22

Dear Father,

I know that I make mistakes and that You promised in Your word that if I repent, which means turn from my wicked ways, You would forgive me. I want to confess my sins and ask for forgiveness for lies of purpose and convenience. I want to speak the truth despite the circumstances and believe I am protected by You. I admit when things look dark or difficult it seems like lying would be more prudent (easier-safer). I want You God to see my love and know that my love for You demonstrates I trust You and am willing to be truthful.

I trust You and being honest will exhibit (show) integrity (goodness) as I represent You. I will not allow the enemy to use my tongue for lies and will not harbor untruths to save face or keep myself from being embarrassed for what I have done. I confess my wrongs and accept Your forgiveness and consequences for what I have done outside of You. It is in this forgiveness I can reconnect with You and be safe. Build in me a clean heart and mind so I might not sin against You. That sin will not keep me from You. My whole life is to please You so I ask You to touch, lead, and guide me, to be honest daily.

In Jesus' Name,
Amen...

Love, "Nick Name"

Notes

Day 13: The Future

An impactful preacher, Joel Osteen, spoke about our story written in God was written with the ending created first. God designates (chooses) our "happy," successful ending and then fills in the beginning and the middle. Since God is the author and finisher, nothing we do is a surprise or thwarts (messes up) what is destined for us. Our future is selected and routed based on our choices and what we are birthed to do.

Some of us will take longer scenic routes to our future while some will take straighter routes. My dad always quoted, "A straight line is the shortest distance between two points." I am a winner not because of what I do, but because of who I am and that I have accepted my chosen status. Surrendering to God, straightened my line to the future, and every day, I try to communicate with God, so I can stay on the straight path. As a child, I was a "fire baby," and things had to be proven to me, but now I am in a hurry to get to my expected end, so I follow the straight line.

Needless to say, I occasionally detour and when I do, I pray and find my way back because God shines a light whether through books, people, situations, or filling my heart. However, when He needs to redirect me, He does because I have a destined future that He created for me. I am always grateful that my story ending is definite and planned because when I get stuck along the path, it gives me hope that God knew I would get stuck here and He already had a plan to help me get "unstuck." You too have a destined future and it is up to you to seek it, walk in it, and believe it despite the obstacles or barriers the enemy places in your path.

Because your future was planned - your escape from the barriers and obstacles are also planned, if you believe and work it out. "Faith without works is dead." Don't tap out! Your end is waiting on you, so keep moving forward.

Scriptures

A. Jeremiah 29:11

B. Proverbs 19:20-21

C. Philippians 1:6

D. Proverbs 3:5-6

E. Proverbs 16:1-4

Dear Father,

To know You know me is reassuring (makes me feel good) - to know You are there for me - to know You love me and have made accommodations for all I will experience on my journey to Your created future is amazing. To know You love me so much You took time to write out every scene in my story is breathtaking. As scenes are written and executed, You make connections to allow me to get back on track.

I thank You for the hope that lies in my life's plan. Each day, I awake with the expectation that You will show up for me - I know You will blow my mind today and You will exhibit Your undying love. I am fully committed to my future, but I get discouraged sometimes. I need reassurance through Your word and through revelations. I want to believe You God and today I pray for You to reference Your word - reinforce Your hand in my life. Open doors which move me closer to my future. Shine Your light on things I need to walk in, on my path to Your future. Continue to lead, guide, and direct me Lord, even when I get complacent and not moving as I should. I ask You God to anoint my "happy" successful end.

In Jesus' Name, I pray.
Amen...
Love, "Nick Name"

Notes

Day 14: School (Education)

Education is one of the most powerful weapons we possess yet it is underestimated daily. One thing that still baffles (shocks) me is the people who use violence and fighting as a way of life overlook the power of the weapon, "education." Many don't realize that education is a weapon; it is a tool of protection as well as for progression. With education and prayer, there is no enemy you cannot overcome and the more education you obtain, the stronger your defense and offense are. When you can use words to determine how people will live in society and use it to tear down unfair abuses, You have power; just as a bullet can take a life so can the law.

Laws, rules, and regulations are all words created based on someone's ideals of what is right and what is wrong. If enough people say something should be done a certain way, (regardless of whether it is right or wrong) that policy may be upheld. What you say or do not say can change a life and eventually the world. Hundreds of years ago - it was lawful to own another person based on their heritage and status in the world. Over the past few years, people have been allowed by law to kill others they felt were unfit to live. No number of guns or weapons can change that. It is the educating of people to what can be done legally to change society's views on equality and the bigotry that could decrease the violence and the killings.

The quote or adage is 'guns don't kill people, people kill people.' This acknowledges that the true weapon is the knowledge of people. We can't fight violence without education. Being educated on the freedoms we have and the issues that affect our ability to unite is the answer to create peace. School is where you arm yourself with the information to survive. It teaches you safety, how to fight, intellectually how to change laws and policies to protect the people. School is how you learn to maneuver in society; where you belong, how your gift can be used to affect your environment and how to bring change when needed. When people use education to change lives, it protects everyone. We are all connected in the beautiful thing we call life. Our relationships are key to winning.

When you have an education, you become powerful and you can dominate your arena. Education builds self-worth, confidence, creates opportunity, and keeps people from taking advantage of you. Then, always protecting what you have, education empowers you to create avenues that will stop others from needing to take it. If everyone is armed with the knowledge of how their life fits in the life cycle/ circle, they become more of an asset and less of a threat. The easiest battle to win is the one you outmaneuver (defeat) your opponent through education. So, the next time you want to challenge yourself, pick up a book, including The Bible, and fill your arsenal (mind) with knowledge of a new topic or idea. You would be surprised how many battles you will win with words backed by ideas and gifted vision.

<u>Scriptures</u>

A. Proverbs 2:6
B. Proverbs 18:15
C. Proverbs 1:7
D. Isaiah 11:2
E. Proverbs 15:14

Dear Father,

Increase my heart for school as my way to deal with life. Though it is not popular to learn, I ask that You touch my mind and fill it with supernatural knowledge. Give me the ability to change my family, neighborhood, and environment with the power of education (the weapon of choice). I know You created knowledge and that You desire us to obtain it. I realize society endorses (promotes; tries to make) ignorance as "cool." My friends make fun of me when I use words that are considered "proper." In some areas it is called talking "white" or they assume I think I am better than them. May I learn something new daily and give me the boldness to share what I learned even if it is not popular. I want to be a warrior for You so I need to know what Your word says and I need the ability to apply it to my life. Allow my presence at school to change things like Joseph.

Give me the desire to be a game changer, a radical (fearless) voice for growth and education. Allow me to lift Your name at school without fear so You can draw my friends and my enemies. That is the only way we all will be able to please You and live a fulfilled life. May my presence at school (my environment) also draw in adults. Allow me to lead Your people with God-led knowledge, and the strength of Your spirit. You God have created me to represent You, so I ask for a fearless pursuit of education and advanced communication for Your glory. Education will make me invincible in You, and I live for that power to grow in You.

In Jesus' Name,
Amen...
Love, "Nick Name"

Notes

Day 15: Heart & Mind

Where is your heart? We pray to imitate David, "a man after God's own heart." But do we feed our heart enough to fulfill that? We don't. We do not take the time out of our day faithfully to feed our hearts with words from God. We read the Bible, but do we meditate on the scriptures? Do you take notes in church when the man/woman of God is ministering and re-read your notes to absorb the word? The Bible says we cannot hear God without the preacher. Do we pray the word when we pray to prove it is in our hearts? The Bible dictates that we study to show ourselves approved "rightly, dividing the word of truth." We cannot do that without knowing the word. Each day we must purposely feed our hearts to be able to live the word and keep our hearts cleansed. It is only with a clean heart that we can hear from God.

We misunderstand the thought that if we do not openly sin, our hearts are clean. But how do we know if we are sinning if we have not held the word in our heart or read the word? The word teaches, fills, builds, rebukes, chastises, invites, soothes, loves, and the enemy tries to gain ground daily. If we study, pray, and fast (abstain from eating for the purpose of connecting with God) the enemy cannot have our mind. Only a small window is needed to establish enough ground to change your heart or stop your progress.

The enemy has no authority, but he can make you give up authority and ground. He will use it to destroy you. Reading, digesting, and walking out God's word is how you prep and protect your mind. There used to be this slogan on TV, "a mind is a terrible thing to waste." I will go further and say a mind blanketed in darkness is worse than death. In death, no one is honored because we are spiritually dead or gone, but in life, a mind that is filled with light saves lives, which honors God, thus, darkness is a form of death. Communicating light bonds us to God.

Without it we are lost, and our hearts are dark. Just as our hearts must be filled with the word so must our mind. We must guard our hearts with the word. If we keep our minds on Jesus, we will protect our hearts with the word. Our mind is where the enemy tries to manipulate us. Emotions and other ideas are used to cloud our mind, so we doubt God, and, in that doubt, we give the enemy authority to dominate our mind and heart leading to our actions. This is how he brings us out of purpose making God a lie and distracting us from the ultimate goal of changing lives, leading them to God. We must endeavor (strive) to keep our mind stayed (focused) on Jesus.

Scriptures

A. *Matthew 6:21*

B. *Romans 12:2*

C. *Proverbs 4:23*

D. *Psalms 26:2*

E. *Philippians 4:7*

Dear Father,

It is my desire, my goal, and my dream to submit my heart and my mind to bring You glory. May every word, deed, and thought demonstrate a surrendered mind and Godly heart. Lord I long to walk in Your image; to speak to Your people with revelation (insight). I see Your will on this Earth in others and I want my heart to be filled with love and word. I want to have a mind of revelation (insight) and one that is lifting You up. My life is to represent You and in doing so, change hearts and minds. May my testimonies exhibit Your hand in my life and confirm my heart is clean and fully surrendered. I awake each day with the idea that I will bring You glory with my life.

It is my reasonable (minimal) service to lift You and Your name to draw people. You sacrificed Your son, so I could be close to You and for that I will serve You. Your people are so filled with outside influences and sinful distractions. You desire that we would all be saved, but without a surrendered heart and mind, that is impossible. Use me to accomplish that goal, Lord. I am grateful that You chose me, and I want to tell everyone. I trust You completely God because You have my mind stayed on You and I know You love me.

Each day I promise to live to bring You glory, and I will stand tall. When I fall short, I will repent. I love You God.

In Jesus' Name,
Amen...

Love, "Nick Name"

Notes

Day 16: Obedience

How many times have you heard that obedience is better than sacrifice? Well, obedience is a requirement as well as a testament to our commitment to God. If we believe He will answer us, He will bless us. He trusts us through our obedience. That is how we prove our heart for God and His will. God needs obedience to allow us to walk in His purpose; our obedience is a choice that is mandatory to connect with God. I know you are asking, "If it is mandatory, how is it a choice?" For example, when your parent says to you, "You better clean your room!" You have a choice. You either choose to do it and not suffer any consequences; maybe even brighten their day, or you could choose to be disobedient and pay the price for not complying (following directions). God gives you free will where you can choose to serve Him, but in the choice to serve Him, obedience is non-negotiable (required).

If you choose to serve God, you are His heir and trusting Him, obeying Him, and His word are required. The Bible says without faith it is impossible to please God. Faith is the result of a trusting relationship and obedience that allows God to operate in your life. If you do not choose Him, He will not operate in your life. Since God is our Creator, He knows us from Alpha to Omega, beginning to end, so obeying Him is a matter of trust. If you believe He created you to reign, to be successful and live an abundant life, you should have no problems obeying Him. But if you chose to allow the enemy to cloud your judgment and plant his falsities in your mind, you will not bond with God as you are designated to and that affects your abilities and your blessings. Everyone looks for control and wanting to direct their own life, but with the uncertainties (difficulties) of life, we can always use assistance in living life. God offers His hand. You are blessed to know God and serve Him. Don't allow the glitter of the fake happiness and alleged better times lure you to death because that is what life without God is, death.

Scriptures

A. Exodus 19:5

B. Deuteronomy 11:1

C. Ephesians 6:1-3

D. II Corinthians 10:5

E. Romans 1:5

Dear Father,

It is hard to be obedient in a world where the mind is always convincing us to be self-indulgent, consumed with materialistic things, and careless about everything. We are taught to mind our business and worry about getting ahead.

The phrase, "self-made" is used to describe a person who has become successful on their own, but in reality has taken their gifts, talents, and opportunities for granted. There is nothing about us that did not come from You. Lord, we are created in Your image and even when we try to stray, it is Your mercy that allows it, and allows Your gift to operate in us. You offer amazing benefits for obedience to You and we will experience supernatural success if we change. Through this change, we become fruit of Your orchard. Without You, God, we cannot experience the fulfillment of You or hope everlasting.

I thank You that my obedience is all You ask for, though You have given me much more than I could ever repay or return. I thank You that I can come to You with my heart open to receive and even when I err, I am still accepted. Use my obedience to draw people to You. Forgive my arrogance and my lack of concern for my fellow man. My obedience is where I get the strength to walk in my calling and without it, many people will lose. Continue to use me as a compass.

Thank You for another chance each day to be used for Your glory. You created me for greatness, and I accept Your choice of me and vow to demonstrate You daily. You chose me and that provides hope and a feeling of belonging. Use me to share the same feelings with my friends and family. Allow me each day to shine for you and forgive me when I fall short. I was created by You. I honor you with my life.

In Jesus' Name, I pray.
Amen...
Love, "Nick Name"

Notes

Day 17: Attitude

Attitudes are feelings or thoughts that can be controlled. How I react to what you say or do, is an example of expressing my attitude. If our attitude goes unchecked our tone, body language, or verbiage (words) can become aggressive, hostile or offensive. When attitudes interfere with our relationships, they cause hurt feelings, strained relationships, and sometimes division.

My aunt sings a song when she feels my cousins and I are allowing our attitudes to go unchecked. "Attitude ... Attitude ... you need to check your attitude." When she sings this, we look at each other and laugh. It helps us realize how petty we are being. When you are putting how you feel above others, you can say and do things that can cause hurt and unforgiveness. God is about growth and love. When you are in a relationship, you must put their heart, feelings, and well-being above your own. If you are earnest (true) in your attempt to engage and work with people, you can overcome many issues, but you must be able to keep your attitude in check. How will you know when your attitude is out of line?

As you talk, read, text, or hear someone talking and you do not agree, you must first ask why you do not agree. Once you know that, it will help you with your response. Take nothing personal if the person you are communicating with is using offensive, demeaning, or tactless (rude) words. They are baiting you and the conversation is generally over, so end it. If they are misunderstanding you or mischaracterizing what you say, try without judgment to redirect the conversation. If they become defensive or accusatory, end the conversation because it will cause your defensive nature to arise.

Conversations can be revisited when calmer minds prevail (when you feel better), but words cannot be unsaid. Your relationship is always worth you double checking your attitude, and people who attack you for their personal gain can be forgiven and then distanced, but you have to maintain control of yourself and your integrity. If you curse or mistreat someone, even if they started it, you are still accountable to God for your action and reaction. You must ask and trust that He will handle the issue and how you portray yourself as a representation of God is the main objective. Always represent God with respect, and He will ensure it is returned one way or the other.

Scriptures

A. Philippians 2:5-11

B. Psalms 51:17

C. Proverbs 15:13

D. Proverbs 17:22

E. Romans 8:7

35

Dear Father,

I long to know I am an asset to the kingdom. By surrendering my heart and mind to You, I give permission for You to dwell in my thoughts and actions. Exhibiting harmful behavior embarrasses and grieves Your spirit. I love You God, and I want to live with my attitude in check. As I speak, as I walk, as I do what I am born to do, I will treat people with the love You have given to me. As a representative of You, made in Your image, I want people to see You as they look at me. It is always my desire to please You and for You to be happy that You created me. I never want You to repent for my creation or look upon me with embarrassment.

God, each day You pour mercy and grace with a helping of blessings and direction for my gifts into me and my life. For the great investment, I try daily to repay Your "wonderfulness." You God have given me so much to share, and I pray You see how much I want to serve, inspire, and love. Forgive me for the times I have carelessly spoken and hurt people because I was angry or hurt and for not seeing Your greatness for the gift that it is. I will never stop striving to give back the heart You have shown me. As You cover me with Your blood, may my attitude reflect Your magnificence. It is my desire to be a "Mini-You" every day!

In Jesus' Name,
Amen...
Love, "Nick Name"

Notes

Day 18: Family

Whether through blood or relationship, family is the core of our existence. God has birthed each of us to a clan that will help us develop. Even when our family is not the best, unsupportive, or not a blessing in our mind, they are contributing to our growth, life, and preparation. They are molding our ability to cope. In the Bible, the tribes had their jobs. The Levites were the priests, so if you were birthed in that tribe, there was an expectation.

In my family, education and serving God in ministries are our identifiers (who we are). Many of us have careers as ministers, teachers, principals, counselors or other areas of education. In the church, we ban together and operate as ministers, pastors, deacons, first ladies, or even bishops.

If you learn your lineage (ancestry), you will find a common thread that should explain why God placed you in that family. Family again can include those in your life that stick "closer than a brother." The idea is to figure out what they are teaching you to prepare you for life. As stated, whether interaction with them is positive or negative, it is a tool to mature you and point you toward God.

God has plans to prosper you and not harm you, so if your family is hurtful it is in those times you are being prepared for your calling. God knows how much we can bear and some of us are given a magnanimous (extremely large) level of sorrow to bear, and it is to build our resiliency (ability to stand), hope, and the use of our gifts. Today, I challenge you to think about what you have learned from family members, even if the relationship is estranged (negative). How can you use the knowledge to bring God glory, so it does not linger in you to root pain and hardship?

Scriptures

A. Ephesians 6:4

B. Colossians 3:13

C. Exodus 20:12

D. Proverbs 22:6

E. Proverbs 6:20

Dear Father,

Today I acknowledge my family is a choice. Though they were not my choice, they were Yours and they were chosen for my destiny, something far beyond my comprehension and my ability to fathom (understand). Open my eyes to what I should learn from them and how I can use the experience to help others and bring You glory.

Touch our relationship and cause myself and estranged (separated) family members to reunite under Your will and Your love. Give us agape (unconditional) love for each other and strengthen the bond we share with You at the center. It is easier sometimes, God, to walk away rather than stand with a loved one and fight for our love. Cause each one in my home/family to commit to being a blessing and to be blessed. Family relationships are for life, so God give us Your spirit. Fill our hearts with Your agenda, Your will, and Your direction. Take away all selfish ideas, thoughts, motives, and/or actions.

Cause us to be on track for You. You, God, are our everything, and so I ask that You protect our family and fill us with peace. You are always working things together for our good, so please open my mind to Your will for my life. Do not allow my petty ideas or emotions lead me astray. I realize I am Your creation and since I cannot change my past or control present pain, give me the strength to trust You and love my family despite issues we encounter (face). Allow me to stand tall and be grateful for all lessons. Cause me to represent You faithfully in all I do.

In Jesus' Name,
Amen..
Love, "Nick Name"

Notes

Day 19: Death

Life is not promised to us outside of the fact that, You will be here if Your salt has flavor (You are contributing your birth gifts and talents to God's work and glory) and second, you honor your parents (guardians) so your days may be long. When people die young, we search, pray, inquire how can this make sense? It is such a waste; they did not get to reach their potential; this cannot be God's will. What we must remember is our end has already been established before we were created. Though we have free will, God still knew our choices before we made them.

It is woven into the fabric of our lives. The choices we make, the life we live, and the way we surrender to God's will all determine the length of our lives. Honoring God's word and His will extends, and the flip side shortens our lives. The wages of sin is death, and that is spiritual death, which can lead to physical death as our lives affect others. Rather than continue to allow us to hurt, lead astray, or damage the future of His children, we are turned over to a reprobate mind and our lives then are surrendered to the enemy. We must be mindful that if we are not in His will, we are not entitled to the promise of a long life.

Additionally, lives are sacrificed also for others. God allows loss of life to save others. This extreme warning is an act of mercy from a Father that would rather us not perish but have everlasting life. As Jesus was sacrificed to re-establish a connection with God, the death of influential youth is a call for others to reconnect before it is too late. Every act on this Earth is orchestrated or allowed for God's glory so if we fully embrace this fact, we can accept His choices above what we would like, how we feel, or what we think is fair. God is about being "Just" and in that, rather than watch His creation suffer physically, mentally, emotionally, and/ or spiritually, He will bring them home to His bosom. Though it is hurtful to us as the outside bystander, we must know the inner workings of the heart and mind of the individual, the relationship they have with their Creator, and what their future holds to comprehend the time of their departure from this world. Death is never a mistake. It may seem like an unfortunate incident, but it is His discretion to extend life daily as life is lent to us based on how it plays part in our purpose.

There is a time to be born and a time to die. We must work while it is day, as when it is dark. .. no man can work. This translates to, work while You are alive as when death comes, work is done. This is not meant to be a message to scare you, but to open Your eyes. When we are young, we think we have all the time in the world to explore, live, make mistakes, and follow our dreams, but we have an appointed time and we must work as though "life is not promised."

Obedience is the key to a long and fulfilled life. Though our time is already calculated, prayer is always an opportunity to ask God for other desires if they are not outside of His will. Live with fulfillment as Your focus, obey Your parents and God's will/word, treat people with love, be mindful that You have an expected end, keep Your judgement to yourself, strive to demonstrate flawless character, and know that as you faithfully utilize your gift(s), God will open more! In that, you will be able to live a long life! Gift upgrade requires more execution time ... Dying is returning to God, which is our finale. We want to return to God because Earth is a temporary placement. The key is to return home as a decorated hero. Reap rewards for your work so You can return home to hear, "Well done my good and faithful servant."

Scriptures

A. Revelations 14:13

B. I Thessalonians 4:13-14

C. Isaiah 57:1-2

D. Ecclesiastes 7:1

E. Romans 14:8

Dear Father,

Death is frightening because we are sometimes unsure of where we are with You and where we will end up. We hear what heaven is like and if we make it in, how magnificent it will be. Nonetheless, we still have doubts and fears because the world portrays death negatively. We question salvation, and if heaven is real because we cannot verify its existence. There is a lot of diversity in religion. There are many questions regarding the difference in religions. How can we achieve everlasting life? Is everlasting life real? Should we worship God, Jehovah, Buddha, or Jesus only? There are so many other differences that divide us as people, I fear that if I die, this will be my end, or I will come back reincarnated as another species.

My only real hope is if I continue to maintain a relationship with You, You will not allow me to go astray. You will lead, guide, and protect me from the outside influences and my own mind that is bombarded by tricks of the enemy to draw me away from You and the truth. I want to be forgiven Lord, so I can return to You. I want to know You have forgiven me. I do not want to wonder if I am in Your will, am I forgiven, or am I able to be used despite my unworthiness.

If I die tomorrow Lord, may I die in Your will, not violently or as a victim of an illness that causes me to suffer. I want to be at peace with You. I want to be at peace with the fact that I will die, and I will die in You. It is Your decision when I will leave this place, so place my heart at peace knowing it will be in my best interest. Give me the strength to live with that ideal and the ability to hold on to Your word. As members of my family, friends, and co-workers pass on, don't allow me to be selfish and dwell in the pain because I did not want to let go. Remind me every death is orchestrated or allowed by You, so it is for good. Comfort my family as we experience death of loved ones, and do not allow depression or any other tactic of the enemy to cloud our hearts and minds as we grieve and then find peace. Make transition of our soul and the end of our destiny, clear to us all so we can celebrate a job well done, just as You do. Remove fear and uncertainty, and fill me with peace and understanding.

In Jesus' Name,
Amen...
Love, "Nick Name"

Notes

Day 20: Faith/Belief

Speaking Faith is a gift that transcends time, situations, and life. As you look at your life and the lives around you, you may not be able to speak faith. Many times, we believe in God, but we do not believe God. That is faith, believing God, taking Him at His eternal word, despite circumstance. In 1996, God gave me the nickname, Faith. Faith is what He calls me. He demonstrates faith through my steps, and I sign my prayers with my nickname signifying our relationship.

It was not clear then as it is now that He gave me that name and that I would have to live like Faith to allow Him to use me in my purpose. Some days, I feel like my name should be Belief, not Faith, as I believe in Him wholeheartedly, yet there are times I do not believe Him. When vision(s) tarry, obstacles overwhelm me, when things I expect do not work out or people around me are flourishing though they have put in what seems like less work, my faith wanes (decreases). I do not have an issue believing He can, it is will He do it? When my situation seems bleak, I pretend to believe to keep from being disappointed, but I am not fooling God. If I do not get my hopes up, and God does not do it, I will not feel bad. Sadly, that is not faith! You see, not getting my hopes up, means I lack faith!

It was not until recently I realized if my name is Faith and I am not living my name, I can plan to fail every time. I was named Faith because I can believe Him on that level, but I must choose to do it. I admit sometimes I do not. I grieve the Holy Spirit with my lack of faith and then cry when things fail or do not go as I believe they should. Today I challenge you to choose. Will you believe Him or just believe in Him? Will you surrender your way to His and live faithfully? I used to be a walking billboard for faith, but now, I am an occasional sign. This day, I take back my faith! The enemy had caused me to suppress it, but no more!!

You too can be a walking expression of God's glory and power, but You must utilize your faith to get there, choose Faith. It is the road to the Supernatural.

Scriptures

A. Mark 11:24

B. Hebrews 11:1

C. James 1:6

D. I Peter 1:8-9

E. II Corinthians 5:7

Dear Father,

I come to You, God, admitting my belief has not blossomed into mature faith. I believe in You because You are all I know. I have felt You, basked in Your love, and seen Your hand upon my life. I have heard You, communicated my heart to You, but somewhere along my journey, I have not nurtured my belief so that it could develop into true faith. Today, I am walking to the next level of belief so that I can manifest the faith to experience supernatural harvest. Having faith in Your word, Spirit, and will for my life is the only way I will operate in the plans and purpose You created for me.

Today, I surrender fully to Your will knowing You have plans to prosper me, and not harm me. I know the result of my life is "I win" because You sealed it with the blood of Jesus. I know I am a victor because Your word says I am more than a conqueror. I realize to be a true Christian (Christ-like) Soul, I must have faith because nothing else pleases You like that - not works, not money, not even obedience. If I have or do all the other things, yet do not have faith, I do not please You. The word said it is "impossible," so I stand on the fact that I have a history with You, and it demonstrates that You deserve my faith. Your word has been evident in my life since birth, and though I have made attempts to trust, I have fallen short.

No more - if I stay connected and allow You to dwell in me and I in You, I will not pray amiss (in vain) and my ministry (what I was birthed to do) will produce harvest. As this occurs, my faith is renewed, strengthened, and becomes a beacon of light to others. I cannot continue to hold-up others because I lack maturity in my faith, so God-anoint me afresh, forgive all lapses in my faith progression and continue to speak to me, so I can remain close to You in Your bosom which is my heart's desire.

In Jesus' Name,
Amen...
Love, "Nick Name"

Notes

Day 21: Sex (Intimacy)

Talking about sex and intimacy used to be "taboo" (inappropriate/unheard of) in church and school settings. Today, there is more freedom, but also more ways to get in trouble or have people complain about views - How does God feel? What is "politically correct" and basically does the church allow real discussion? I remember my first year as a middle school science teacher. Sex education was a part of the curriculum. I had to send home permission slips before I could discuss the contents of the book. The form told parents that Sex Ed was mandatory to inform students about the "science" of sex, childbirth, hormones, diseases, sex organs, and anything that dealt with how sex affected your body.

It was scary because I did not want to promote promiscuity (having sex with several people outside of a marriage) by giving facts with experiences. I also couldn't express my spiritual views or my parental concerns. I had to stick to the "science" and anyone who knows me knows that was asking the impossible. Nothing about sex is just scientific or without personal communication. I needed to be able to express the emotional component, so if these young people chose to move into that realm, they would understand the consequences, the joys (for married people) and the effects/consequences of the decision. Sex is about connection and without the full picture, people could make errorneous life-altering decisions.

I found out that sex was so relationally involved that there are even legal circumstances dealing with it created to explain murder. It is called crime of "passion," which I linked to the intimacy of sex and relationships. If they had to include this in a defense for people accused of violence and murder, then there would be more to this phenomenon (extraordinary act) than just scientific rhetoric (word, terms, and ideas). When married people are caught in the sex act with someone other than their spouse (husband or wife), the violence that ensues (occurs) is a crime of "passion." Sex is the bonding of two people. It is used in scripture to allow a man and a woman to become one and the love that is exchanged, now can lead to the production of another life. This is God's plan - that a man and woman come together, become one, and reproduce. It is how God brings His purpose to pass through the lives created. God wants us to have children, so they can be raised to love, praise, and serve. Once two people have bonded through the intimacy that is sex, they have given their most precious gift to the other person.

Therefore, it is saved for marriage because the act is the most vulnerable (open) state you can be in. It is important to guard yourself against giving yourself to people unworthy of the commitment. Sex exposes your physical body to dangers that can affect your systems and cause incurable illnesses or fatality (death). On the emotional front, if you give yourself to someone on this level, you believe your heart is connected to theirs, and if they do not feel the same, then it can cause conflict deep enough to affect your heart, mind, body, and soul. Sex leads to physical and emotional expectations. It can cause such despair that individuals can contemplate (think about) or commit suicide. There are apps, websites, and movies that portray promiscuity (sex with several people) as connections that are interchangeable (move or replace each another). They make these inappropriate (ungodly) acts exciting. They make you believe it is okay to change partners, engage in group acts, view sex as a sport, and give yourself to as many people as you please. Sadly, indulging in the negative aspects and "pleasures" of promiscuity, you do not realize the lie that has been told until you are deep into the deception and inevitable depression of it all. Sex can breed life, bring hope and connections, or devastating chaos. It is all determined by the motives of the people participating in the act and how they understand the purpose of sex. Remember you are God's most precious creation, and when you choose to give yourself to someone else through sex, it needs to be someone chosen by God to connect with, not just physically, but emotionally, and spiritually because whether you admit it or not, that is what you are doing. You have chosen to become one with that individual and God desires that oneness to last a lifetime, not just one night. So, choose wisely as it is one of the most important decisions you will ever make.

Scriptures

A. I Corinthians 6:18

B. I Thessalonians 4:3-5

C. Genesis 2:24

D. Hebrews 13:4

E. I Corinthians 6:9

Dear Father,

Thank you for the opportunity to find, give, and receive love because You are love. You created a way for us to bond with another person, so we would not be alone, and we could celebrate our love through intimacy. I understand You have a purpose for me, and I cannot subject myself to anyone that would jeopardize that. I don't want to view sex as lightly as the world.

I want to understand what it is and how it will affect me. I want to only give myself to the man or woman You choose. I will not let society trick me into believing that freedom to have sex if I please is what You planned for me. I will pray and with Your guidance, decide what is right for my life. When we bond, it will be after marriage and until death do us part as You have designed. I am grateful You thought enough of me to give me direction on this life altering (changing) act. Thank you God for giving me love to fill my heart as I wait on the partner You created for me. Thank You for loving me enough to allow me to unite with another and become one for your glory, honor, and purpose.

In Jesus' Name,
Amen...
Love, "Nick Name"

Notes

Day 22: Peer-Pressure (Fitting in)

Friends are usually responsible for how we feel about life, society, and ourselves. Their opinions of us as a person, as well as our accomplishments, our failures, and our decisions affect how we live, operate, and progress. Peers can make or break our self-worth, so the amount of "stock" (belief) we place in their words must always be judged. What your peers think of you is not always linked to you or what you do. Sometimes envy, fear, misunderstandings, or a lack of seeing your purpose (what we were created to do) lead to what people think about you.

These perceptions can bring light, but also may cause you to be ashamed. It is not your fault. It is a fight waged by the enemy because he does not want you to fulfill your purpose or bring glory to God through your life. Each day you must be prepared to use your gift to help others despite how you feel or what people say. Your peers, if they are truly your friend, will build you up, give you encouragement, and tell you the truth even if you might not want to hear it.

Constructive criticism builds you up, it does not tear you down. If your peers try to convince you to do something that is not beneficial to you, do not do it. Unfortunately, people are interested in entertaining themselves by watching you suffer. Occasionally, they will advise you to do things that are not right, so they can seem like a better individual than you. The enemy uses people, which is the only way he can attack you, and regrettably, people do not realize they are being used. They may even convince themselves they are helping you. Though it sounds hurtful, sometimes people hurt others because they have been hurt.

It is your job to make good decisions and learn from obstacles, so you can help others. Life is about influencing other people and ideas to change the world for God's glory. We all have a piece of life we can affect, but it is up to us to take full advantage of our gifts to do so. Don't allow your life to be stunted or placed in a box by peers who do not know what they have to offer the world so they want to keep you from offering anything as well. You are blessed to change lives, so walk in it without fear! Only God's opinion counts in the end, and if He is pleased, you are where you should be, offering what He has given you to offer the world.

Scriptures
A. Genesis 19:9
B. Luke 23:23
C. Matthew 14:9
D. Psalms 55:3
E. Isaiah 16:4

Dear Father,

Thank You for another day. Thank You for life, health, and strength. Thank You for blessing me and my life. Thank You for being with me and teaching me what I need to move in my purpose. God, I thank You for my peers and as they speak to me, give me discernment to know what to receive from them. I know some will be in my life to support and some will be in my life to push me closer to You as they try to distract me. Open my heart and mind to their intentions and allow me to see what I should gather from them. Your word provides hope, comfort, direction, and protection.

Bless those that bless You and protect me from those who would try to keep me from following Your will and Your word for my life. Show me how I can lead them to You. Cause me to lift Your name so You can draw them in. Cause me to be a holy and Godly example of You. Allow me God to bless Your people with my words and my faith. Guide me to make solid decisions and to exhibit Your love everywhere I go. My life long desire is to please You. I love You despite circumstance and how people treat me. I will continue to distinguish Your will from my own, and as I walk closer to You, make my life an example of success and love.

In Jesus' Name,
Amen...
Love, "Nick Name"

Notes

Day 23: Money (Provision)

"Money is the root of all evil." This is a Bible statement people quote incorrectly. It is the "love" of money that is the root of all evil. When you place money above God, that is sin. We should love God as God is love and our Father; our greatest connection should be with God and His image. Money answereth (addresses) all things, so God believes in money and provision. What we cannot allow is money to become an idol or something to praise or worship. God has provided us with gifts to obtain wealth. If you follow His principles, you will find prosperity is high on the list of promises. God promises to provide if You tithe and give offerings. He promises to bless your storehouse and your wallet if you are obedient.

God promises He will rebuke the devourer for His namesake, so I would say He wants us to have abundance. Through our hands, God provides for us as we surrender our money to Him for Him to expand, extend, and bless. If we are operating with closed fists, trying to hold on to the little money we earn, we cannot receive more. As we do not always have good, fruitful intentions, we must allow God to direct us. Many will risk money on the stock market with investments, but complain about supporting the church.

Money is a way to show God's love and to offer support, so we can fulfill His will in this world. Therefore, He must provide for us to be able to use it for ourselves and others. When we are used to answer prayers, for example, when we give money to a stranger who needs an operation, we represent God's love and provision for His people. This show of love may be the very act that turns people back to God. There are times when we give up on God, life, and ourselves because we feel we cannot take any more and then God sends a glimmer of hope through another person, rekindling the spark in our hearts.

Before you give into the false stories and temptation to spend your tithe and offering on other means, be reminded that God's provision is eternal (promised for life) and has contingencies (requirements) because He has a proven method of success that He directs. It also limits your options or blessings by making wrong decisions with your money. Abundance (more) is a promise of God's word. We should never think we have answers outside of God. He should always be able to direct and use us for His glory!

Scriptures

A. Deuteronomy 28:2-6

B. Luke 6:34-36

C. I Timothy 6:10

D. Proverbs 13:11

E. Ecclesiastes 7:12

Dear Father,

I thank You for provision. I thank You for loving me enough to fill me with a gift that can make room for me and can enable me to obtain wealth. I am grateful that You love me enough to promise me the option to choose to give. I want to give because You gave to me. I want to be an extension of You for others. The fact that I am a lender and not a borrower is amazing and decided by You.

I am so excited about how much You have committed to Your children and how we can look to You for direction and support. I love being supportive for others as it proves I am blessed. God, I pray I would always make You proud with my life choices and my financial practices. I pray for Your hand to steer me in using my money responsibly, and I pray that You would trust me with this and more as I demonstrate my faithfulness and desire to be an example to others. I will strive each day God to give Your people what You have placed in me to change and bless their lives. I will not forsake You as You are my first love. Thank You God for choosing me to go out and speak Your word and help Your people. May my money transcend the natural and operate supernaturally for others, my family, and me.

In Jesus' Name,
Amen...
Love, "Nick Name"

Notes

Day 24: Resilience... "Don't Tap out"

Over the summer, I stay up all night and watch Netflix because I can do what they call "binge watching." I watch episode after episode of shows I have missed out on during the school year. One of the shows I enjoy is a story of two girls who have experienced years of abuse at the hand of foster parents, abandoning parents, and the world they live in. Despite their dark upbringing, they fight to stay together and use their gift as vocalists to pursue their dreams of singing.

On the last episode I watched, the lead character of the show says no matter what she endures she will not "tap out." That stood out to me because I feel the same way. I believe despite how the enemy tries to distract me emotionally, physically, mentally, spiritually, or financially, I will not "tap out." I will use my gifts even when people are trying to oppress me. If people try to attack me about things, if my peers criticize me, if others try to convince me that I belong where they feel I should be, and even when the answer I want from God is delayed, I do not give in, I do not quit, I do not "tap out." I stand on God's word.

I believe His promises. I walk out my purpose where I am, and I pray for my next blessing to manifest (show-up). It is not easy. I cry at times, I consider getting out of His will, by doing my own thing. I even talk trash as if I can move God with my words, but despite it all, I stick to His promises and I work on my character every day. I don't allow my desires to supersede (overtake) God's plan and even when I am ostracized (people turn their backs on me) for sticking to what God has said, I stand.

I am chosen to represent God on this Earth, I am the answer to many issues and wherever I am, my gift is the solution to the issues there. I know man tries often to take credit for my brilliance and for placing me in places to draw an answer from me, but I am God made - not man made, and my perfection is the result of His planning, even before I was born. It's so amazing that I am so loved and that He planned to choose me before I was even created. God created me and then placed me, despite my flaws, to impact His creation. I think about this fact every time I am tempted to "tap out." Then I smile, and I tell the enemy, "I don't tap out! Period.

Scriptures

A. Habakkuk 3:17

B. Psalms 31:23-24

C. I Thessalonians 5:16-18

D. Philippians 4:13

E. Ephesians 6:10-14

51

Dear Father,

Thank You for creating me with everything I need to be successful for You God. You take me to another level every time, and I show You that You can trust me even when things don't go as I envision (see). You update my vision and give me what I need to be supernatural where I am. When You are ready, You promote me, and I am grateful. I thank You that I can lean on You and despite how the enemy attacks, I am not destroyed. I may be wounded at times, but I'm restored to an even better state afterwards. Help me trust You fully. Show me how to come to You with power to receive Your anointing and walk tremendously in the spirit. My resilience is the by-product (result) of our relationship. It has built my faith and powers my quest to constantly upgrade. I look to You for more. I need You to propel me to the next level because I am eager to walk in purpose - Your purpose. Gird (support) me with Your strength and love so I can resist the temptation to stay on one level or give up when tough times come to my door. Thank You for how You extend Your hand over my life and move me forward. I am because You live!

In Jesus' Name,
Amen...

Love, "Nick Name"

Notes

Day 25: Health

Good health is God's desire. Jehovah Rapha is whom you pray to when you need healing. Attacking our health is one of the ways the enemy tries to distract us or cause doubt, so we will not move, and I give thanks to God for the promise of healing. With purpose and surrendered love, we are a powerful weapon against the enemy. The enemy's strategies are simple. If he cannot get you mentally or spiritually, he will send problematic diagnoses, diseases, exhaustion and other issues that will break you down. The great thing is God promises, "No weapon formed against [us] shall prosper."

This includes health issues. When we hear words such as cancer, lupus, or HIV, we hear a death sentence. We know God can heal anything, but we still become fearful. Sometimes we know God can, but doubt that He will because we know other friends, family members, or people who have died from the same illness so if God didn't save them, maybe He won't save me. Despite all of that, God also has His hands all over our situations. What we eat, drink, and how we treat our bodies has bearing on our health, but it does not have the final say.

Do you get enough rest, exercise, or take care of yourself mentally? Stress is one of the most fatal issues we face leading to diabetes, high blood pressure, strokes, heart attacks, and often fatality (death). These elements can be controlled through prayer. We can ask God to show us how to take care of ourselves and follow His word. The Bible instructs us to cast our cares on Him.

This is the number one answer to good health. When you feel well mentally and spiritually, you will strive to care for yourself physically. Eating healthier is a choice we can make every day. Our decision should be to take preventative measures because once we are forced on a diet due to poor health, it makes it more difficult to maintain as it becomes emotional as well as physical. This eventually leads to more stress, which causes additional health problems. Anything we experience in our health is at the discretion of God for His glory, so we pray for God to have His way and in doing so, we ask Him to touch our situation.

Scriptures

A. Corinthians 6:19-20

B. Deuteronomy 7:12-15

C. III John 1:2

D. Proverbs 17:22

E. Jeremiah 33:6

Dear Father,

I am grateful for my relationship with You. As I grow closer to You, I give You permission to lead, and guide. I direct my life in that commitment. I can experience true joy because You will address my mind, body, and soul. As I surrender my health concerns to You Lord, I look for healing. I speak to my body to be under Your control. My flesh is subject to my spirit man (Your Spirit) as God, You are a spirit and my Creator. I pray for Your will in my life, so my body might be under Your direction in order to fulfill my purpose.

As I follow You, take care of me. I pray that I will feel myself getting more and more strength. I am thankful for a Father who takes care of me mentally, emotionally, spiritually, and physically. Touch me Lord from the crown of my head to the soles of my feet. I rebuke the spirit of illness and disease. I break any generational curses that are trying to pass through me by the blood of Jesus Christ. I know the enemy uses DNA to pass disease onto families, but by the blood of Jesus I bind those elements from my life and the lives of my family. My health will not control me or my destiny. It will not keep me from the pursuit of You and all Your glory. My body is fully submitted to You Lord today!!!

In Jesus' Name,
Amen. . .
Love, "Nick Name"

Notes

Day 26: Responsibilities

Being responsible for things is a great honor, but rarely do people see it positively unless they desire to be a leader. When we are assigned duties or asked to hold onto items for safekeeping, our hearts start to change. We are concerned because we don't either want the   responsibility, or we are afraid to disappoint the people who have given us the responsibility. It is nothing like the feeling of failure or the fear of humiliation resulting from not meeting   expectations.   Life is full of chances to succeed or fail, but in our ability to ignore our fears, doubts, and shame to walk in our gifts, we overcome and shine.

We are responsible for ourselves, our neighbors, and to move forward in God despite distractions, negativity and unexpected circumstances, and despite the voices inside of us that echo what others say, "You can't, you won't, you aren't, or you shouldn't." We are responsible to navigate life on our own terms as God created us to do. He made us unique with a specific quality to reach specific people.

Your ultimate responsibility is to be true to the call. Chosen people must be honest with themselves that the responsibility seems overwhelming and impossible to fulfill, but they know they are nothing without the call. Even when we hide from responsibility it sneaks up   on us and runs us down because it is the very fabric we are made from.   We have responsibilities and denying them is an insult to God. When we deny them, we are telling Him He got it wrong. We can't possibly be who He wants to handle things, as if He doesn't know who we are, what we have done, and what we are made of. The area you are responsible for was why you were created. The problem, issue, or concern was introduced in the atmosphere and you were birthed to address it, so wear responsibility like you know it called you!

Scriptures
A. Romans 14:10-12

B. II Corinthians 6:3

C. Galatians 6:4-5

D. Romans 14:15-16

E. II Peter 1:10

Dear Father,

We live our lives searching for fulfillment. One day we feel like we have achieved much, yet if we are still here, we still have more fulfillment to acquire. I remember wondering if I was enough. How can I do it? What if it doesn't work? I don't want to be responsible for others.

It was then that I learned words from the pastor, how can I think I know better than the Alpha and Omega, the beginning and the end? How can I question the very magnificence that breathed His Spirit into me? You are a wonderful father who solves problems through my life.

You are God. The same God who without a thought, orchestrated (planned) thousands of events since the beginning of time to ensure I would be in the right place at the right time. How can I fathom (understand) Your ways and how You use such an imperfect (flawed) soul? I'm glad Your provision for the elements of this world include the production of a perfect answer in an imperfect person, which is me. Each day I decide to surrender who and what I am to Your glory.

Please accept my flawed personage (self) as a covenant to extend You in this imperfect world. I will be responsible for sharing Your love, demonstrating Your heart, and walking in Your purpose for Your glory. I am responsible for searching for direction and with that responsibility, I will walk upright for You every day!

In Jesus' Name,
Amen...
Love, "Nick Name"

Notes

Day 27: Blended Family

Family is created from birth for our assignment. The various situations in families extend beyond bloodline. Without DNA connections, sometimes people can draw invisible lines that separate themselves from those they need to reach their destiny. They may or may not accept help, disciplining or love from these people even though they are family, so it makes it even more difficult if there are additions to the family called extended family.

Stepparents must work hard to fit in with an already established family. They struggle for inclusion, respect and love that is associated with the family. Stepchildren feel less loved, less connected because they see themselves as an outsider. When that occurs, stepchildren often rebel to avoid feeling unloved. They believe if they are rejected because of behavior, that it is better than being rejected just because they are not born in the family. On the other end of the spectrum, some overcompensate (try too hard to be liked), so the surrogate siblings (stepbrother(s)/sister(s)) resent their "kiss up," perfect behavior. This causes fights, both verbal and sometimes physical and parents become torn. They are connected by DNA and love to one and committed to the other due to a love relationship. The tear that is exaggerated (extended) through these fights, divides the family and if not addressed, it will seem like family members are trying to offer love or more love to someone from the outside.

Blended families include two different families trying to bind together under one roof. These families are doing so through marriage, but they need to be joined emotionally as well. They need to be ushered into a family relationship, not one day it is three family members, then the next day there are six family members. That is asking a lot. Because love conquers all, it can be worked out. Families usually feel things will eventually work out, but if not handled directly, the anger builds into hatred and can escalate to acting out violently, running away, abuse/neglect, or death/suicide. Additionally, family members or guardians may be assigned to children to care for them when a parent cannot.

The sad part though is the guardians stepping in to provide for the child/children sometimes are subjected to the anger, frustration, or fear the youth cannot express towards their biological family. "You are not my mother/father" is a familiar statement when children get upset with policies enforced by their guardians. When working with them, I present these scenarios, so they can look on either side of the situation. When dealing with people, there are other points of views to consider. If we never put ourselves in another person's shoes when we are explaining, disciplining or arguing, then we cannot grow, learn, or ensure we are being heard. People don't listen to people who don't listen. As an influencer, you must first listen! In listening, you find yourself and the connection to others. Parents, brothers, sisters, blended families, and guardians all increase the love in our lives by various means.

57

If we never embrace them, we will never be able to benefit from the love and gift God has placed in them. God allows families to come together in various forms for love or to address the lack of love. We have free will, so when families are re-created, God will utilize (use) the opportunity despite how it came to occur, to work for our good.

That is a promise He made us. We may not get along or there may be issues that happen in the new family that are not appropriate, but it was allowed by God for growth. We must remember God is a "gentle spirit" that does not force His will upon us. When evil transpires (happens), it is because man is exercising their will over God's plan. It is up to us to learn from what happens and place ourselves in a position to be protected. Do not allow fear of what may happen direct your path or block you from forming a bond with a newly formed family.

Scriptures

A. Matthew 10:11-13

B. Colossians 3:18-20

C. Proverbs 31:27

D. Genesis 47:12

E. Joshua 6:25

Dear Father,

We all have "adopted" family members such as "play" cousins, brothers, and other individuals who we call family. I pray for them today. Your word says You will stick closer than a brother. This relationship teaches me that You are merciful, loving, kind, and extremely tolerant. Without extended family, people can be subjected to living in foster care homes or shelters. Though we don't always get along with our siblings, I thank You for the difference as that is the answer to progression. We can still love them and grow in acceptance.

Cleanse my heart Lord, so I can love even when I don't understand or get along with the new family that is formed through marriage and not DNA. Keep me from judging and having a leery (uneasy) attitude. In my imperfect fleshly body, I know I may be tempted to dislike selfishly because I do not want an addition to my family or life. I want to represent You with everyone in my life and walk in purpose.

So, touch my heart today. You chose me to be a part of this family and I want to trust Your decision. Keep me from thinking I know better. Do not allow me to hold my heart captive. I need Your direction in how to accept people that can potentially hurt or leave me. I do not want to continue to hold on to the hurt of losing previous family members, but I cannot let go without help from You Lord. I need You to touch my heart God, please. I am living for You and wish to extend Your love to all I encounter.

In Jesus' Name,
Amen...
Love "Nick Name"

Notes

Day 28: Abuse

Cases of abuse are extremely prevalent (numerous) in society. Abuse is not just physical, but mental, emotional, and spiritual. Abuse is on the rise. The way adults treat you, each other, and even animals have abuse levels at an all-time high. The name-calling, yelling, and humiliation, even on professional jobs have skyrocketed and have drawn the nation's attention. There are alarming statistics and articles highlighting how people are abused.

Even the President of the United States, Donald Trump, exemplifies verbal abuse daily by name calling, posting disrespectful "Tweets," degrading women, speaking to and about the press negatively, and commenting about people of other countries in derogatory ways. Schools have trainings and group counseling to let the youth know that if they are being abused, whom they can contact for help and support. When encountering physical abuse, we can call the police, so who do you call when your church has hurt you?

The actions, demeaning comments, and manipulation for monetary gain does exist though churches never want to admit it happens in their congregation. I have witnessed church leaders use of degrading language, defeating tones, and abusive authority to manipulate their leaders to meet expectations and financial requirements. They try to make the congregation and especially the leaders feel guilty if they do not give or if their living is not up to their standard. They do all of this under the guise (umbrella) of "tough love." They try to insinuate it is God's way or His requirement when they have their own agendas to fulfill. They may raise their voice, throw tantrums, make offensive comments, and tell people what to do with their money.

God is a God of love. He does not condemn His people. He does hold them to standards, and He expects His chosen to follow, and obey their master's on Earth, but embarrassing them in public to make them attend church or give offering is not His voice. When you feel like your home church is abusing the relationship, you must pray to get guidance. God has you where you are to receive something, so you need to realize what you need to receive so you can grow up. You must form a relationship with your church leaders, so when you feel like you are being hurt you can get clarity because there are times when we misinterpret what people are saying or doing.

If they are unwilling to work with you, you need to ask God what step to take next. All people are human and make mistakes, but it is the willingness to work it out and change that tells you if you are dealing with Christian character. Discernment is a necessary gift that is a crucial component in knowing God's heart, and if the people in your stratosphere (environment) are walking the Christian walk with you.

Scriptures

A. Hebrews 13:3

B. I Corinthians 7:15

C. II Timothy 3:1-8

D. Ephesians 4:31-32

E. Romans 12:18

Dear Father,

I am hurting. I feel disrespected, discounted, unappreciated, and unworthy. I don't want to continue this way. Help me communicate first by praying, so I can be transparent (open). I need You, God, to show me what to do about the issues that I encounter that hurt me. I need You to protect me from those that will hurt me physically, mentally, emotionally, and spiritually. Open my eyes to see who is intentionally hurting me. Remove me from situations that are not character building and those who would abuse me for their gain, to boost their ego, or to distract me from my goals. God, cause my tolerance to be strengthened by Your hand and cast down spirits of superiority in my peers that would ignite abuse. I rebuke that abusive spirit from my family, friends, teachers, administrators, church members, and leaders through the blood of Jesus.

If I am abusing anyone God, redirect me. Cause me to see, hear, and change how I treat them as I want to represent You and Your love. I pray they would forgive me when I offer my apology and free their soul from unforgiveness for what I have done. Use me to restore and empower people away from abuse. I will not be a victim of any kind of abuse as I am a child of God, and I will walk as such. Thank You God for protecting me from it all. May everyone who deals with me be a blessing and far from abusive. I bind abuse in my life through the blood of Jesus.

In Jesus' Name,
Amen...
Love, "Nick Name"

Notes

Day 29: Choices

"If she says one more word, I'm going to curse her out." That sounds like words from a reality show. Watching reality TV can be an eye-opener or curse, depending on how you look at the show and what you take away from it. Drinking alcohol before or after twenty-one, smoking cigarettes or having unprotected sex are all choices. You may not know the effects of these choices until it's too late. Whether we acknowledge it or not, we make life altering choices daily, and we do not get enough information or experience before we make these difficult choices. The Bible is a handbook of living life. It tells us how good, appropriate choices bless us and how ill prepared (uninformed) choices bring about pain and damnation at the worst. For that reason, you should create a model for making decisions. With me, I do not do anything that does not benefit me in one mode or another. Writing a children's series of books has blessed me with purpose such as the ability to give financial blessings to youth, provide learning opportunities, and operate in the realm of impactfulness.

Though I don't benefit from it directly, I am able to find pride in the copies sold and joy in the fact that I help raise scholarship money. Additionally, families express how happy their children are about *The Adventures of Sherrie and Chubbie*, and that warms my heart. It demonstrates that when you walk faithfully in your gift, God will open more gifts because He knows He can trust you. If the book did not earn money for scholarships, did not sell, or did not impact people, there would be no reason to continue, but because it has provided benefits for hindered children, it was a good choice and I will continue for the rest of my life.

Ask yourself before you make a choice, what does this choice bring to enhance my life or the lives of others? If it is not beneficial to anyone, another choice should be made. Many choices are not changeable and can't be taken back so an analysis (evaluation) before implementation (doing something) is a prerequisite (requirement) for any choice.

Scriptures

A. I Corinthians 10:13

B. John 7:17

C. II Peter 3:9

D. Galatians 5:13

E. Joshua 24:15

Dear Father,

It is my heart's desire to make choices that please my family and You. If what I am contemplating (thinking about) will not bring You joy, help me adjust. God guide me in Godly thoughts, actions, and feelings. I want to be with You and because You want that, You created me in Your image. When that strategy failed, because man gave up his authority to the enemy by disobeying You, You made the choice to sacrifice Your son for me, so we could reconnect, bond, communicate, and I will live my life for You. I choose to love You.

I choose to surrender my life to You. I choose to be accountable for my choices and I choose Lord to follow You despite the journey. Anoint me afresh so I can be confident in my choices. Fill me with discernment, so when I make decisions they are based on truth and not falsehoods. Adjust my life so that I can walk with You not as Your servant but as an heir and have people come to You because of Your calling on my life. The most amazing choice I have made in my life is to surrender and follow You - may my heart remain true, everlasting to everlasting.

In Jesus' Name,
Amen...
Love, "Nick Name"

Notes

Day 30: Friendship

I saw a quote today that, "you can be friends with someone for years and it could take years before you realize that they were never your friend." So, in this quote I saw myself. I realized that I value friendship differently than others and because of that I have not had many true friends. A friend has a mutual stake (joined interest) in the success of the relationship. They understand you most of the time, they can tell you anything, even when you are wrong, and they are just as invested in your success as you are because you honor each other. A friend cries when you cry, laughs when you laugh, and gets on your case when you are performing below your gift. They don't take other people's word about you without hearing your side, and they do not allow anyone to harm you no matter who it is. A friend loves you.

People mistake associations and working relationships for friendships and they turn positive relationships into dysfunctional situations when they do not have enough love to offer an exchange. A friend will not blame or become jealous of how your life evolves. When you are speaking to your friends, please notice behaviors, comments, and topics of discussion. These are signs of friendship. When they are negative, tear people down, and make fun of people, this is not a true friend. They may be unhappy with their life and not be willing to be a friend to you because you are not struggling or are thriving despite life situations. Nothing shows the true color of friendship like success.

Friendship is a beautiful gift from God. It allows us to exhibit love and concern for people. Good friends support each other and inspire each other to higher levels. Friends also foster hope. They remind you of how you can turn to God for everything, with prayer and building confidence. God calls us "friend" so He honors friendship and desires us to be friends with other believers to strengthen our walk and encourage growth. Friends don't judge you because they know you're with them and they accept you as you are, allowing you to be yourself and move your friendships with God above all else. There is an old cliche' (saying) stating, to have friends, you have to show yourself friendly.

Scriptures

A. Corinthians 15:33

B. II Kings 2:2

C. Job 2:11

D. Luke 6:31

E. Proverbs 18:24

Dear Father,

Thank You Lord for friendship. Friendship is a gift from You. You ordered it and moved me from servant to friend. I pray that I would be a Godly friend. I want to be a blessing to those that choose to call me friend. I pray that my words and deeds would represent Your heart and concern. I want to give my friends support and unconditional love. I ask for discernment (wisdom and revelation about people) to choose friends that are of good character and will love me as well.

I know we should help each other, so I want to be an example and have a friend to grow with. As we move through life, we can depend on each other for advice, communication, and fun times. Life is difficult, so I pray for someone to share and progress with. Keep me from being judgmental and high-minded. I pray for our protection from bullying and hurting each other. Keep our mouths from speaking guile (negativity) and using our tongue to speak death rather than life. May my friendships be blessed and productive. I am grateful to You Lord for those friendships and the friendship I have with You.

In Jesus' Name,
Amen...
Love, "Nick Name"

Notes

Day 31: Love & Hate

Society says that there is a thin line between love and hate and that is because our emotions can lead us one way or the other. Love is of God; hate is of the devil. The devil hates us and God because of jealousy and vanity. If you do not allow yourself to indulge (participate) in those emotions, hating people is not possible. God hates behaviors not people. So, we too must model this. You can hate what someone does without hating them. I hate evil and sin because it destroys lives, but I don't hate the sinner. I get angry and sometimes I am tempted to argue with people, but arguments end up with me having to apologize and I hate that more, especially if someone started with me. This causes me to pray more and talk less. I will speak my truth, reiterate (repeat) it with details and then leave it to God. I have found that prayer allows me to be honest but not go too far. We can't try to represent God at 9:00 a.m. but then "fuss" at people at 10:00 a.m. I do stand up for what is right, confronting evil and inequality, but I don't allow people to cause me to go too far because once you have, you cannot take it back.

The Bible talks about living peaceful with everyone as much as possible as people are human and flawed, so it is not always possible. I take a step back and pray and let God deal with the issue. I find He works it out for our good because it is how we reach people for His glory. We may be the only example someone sees of God so we must be malleable (able to shape) with integrity and unconditional love. God loves every time we can work things out, turn the other cheek, and demonstrate good character despite how we are treated. Forgiveness is His way. When we demonstrate good character, we make God real to people. How we handle adversity (obstacles or issues) establishes love. There are times when we will be hated because of who we are, what we do, whom we belong to, and how we handle it is vital (important) to God's will. Do not hold people's shortcomings against them as we would not want ours held against us. Sometimes we are offensive to people in name and deed without knowing it, so we must ensure we communicate with love and when we feel ourselves becoming angry - stop, regroup, and communicate again. No one wants to be disrespected or abused so if you don't want to give place to hate you have to temper (control) your words, actions, and deeds. Your words can determine who you are in the minds of people, so create a loving image just like Jesus.

Scriptures

A. Luke 6:32

B. I John 2:9-17

C. Ephesians 4:31

D. John 13:35 & 14:15

E. Proverbs 8:13

Dear Father,

Love is the object of my goals. I desire to love and to be loved. I realize that hate is a natural response to being mistreated, but it is not of You. You are love and I too am love because I was created in Your image, so there is no place in my heart for hate. Cleanse my heart from all hate, and keep me from becoming prey to feelings and thoughts that bring about hate. I will love my enemies as much as my friends because You, God, love everyone. Obedience is better than sacrifice, so equip me to be able to extend Your love to everyone.

Allow me to shine through everything I say and do. I am grateful for Your love and support that You have given me, and I pray You will continue to use me as a symbol of Your love for Your people. Cause me to be worthy to be used and use me to love everyone. I rebuke the spirit of hate from my heart and life. Love is my only choice because I am Your creation; created in Your image. Through Your heart for me, I ask You to continue to bless me with supernatural, unconditional love.

In Jesus' Name,
Amen...

Love, "Nick Name"

Notes

Bonus: Thank You

There are times when I just want to Thank God. I do not want to ask for anything, remind Him of my worries, or discuss my heart. I just want to take the time out to say thank You. I need God to know how important He is to me, my life, and all that I am. I want God to feel my heart. I know I cannot live without Him, and He must know how grateful I am for all He has done. The older generation says if God does not do anything else for them, they will be content. They express that they have gotten so much love, wisdom, knowledge, and understanding, as well as so many miracles so far along in their walk, that if God does not lift another Holy finger to help them, they will still give Him praise and glory!

Today, I love Him for all He has birthed in me, and I am looking forward to future endeavors (accomplishments, moves). I realize being surrendered to God is where I will continue to thrive, so I spend time just to acknowledge His amazing nature and being there with Him. I am nothing without God and for that I will be eternally grateful. Praise is where I live!

Scriptures
A. Chronicles 16:34

B. Colossians 3:15-17

C. I Timothy 4:4-5

D. Psalms 30:12

E. Philippians 4:6

Dear Father,

Today, I focus on praising You. I offer thanksgiving to You and praise Your name. I want You, God, to stand with me, and I want to dwell with You. Today, I do not seek anything but the chance to acknowledge how awesome You have been, how You have changed my life, and how You have touched me. As You look over my life, I want You to smile with pride. I want You to know I see how much You have done for my family and me.

As we commune (come together), I need You to feel my heart. I cannot make it in this world without You. I would not be as far along as I am without Your mercy, grace, gifting, love, and operation in my life. I strive to honor You, who You are and what You have created me to do.

I know God I am Your representative on Earth, and I thank You for choosing me. I thank You for allowing me the chance to repent each time I fail You. Thank You for honoring my cries in the midnight hours, and answering my prayers despite my failures. I am grateful You love me, and I am so amazed at how You have touched my family and everything I put my hands to. You are a God of promise and for Your undying commitment to me, I thank You. God, You have shown me that I am capable of love, change - capable of forgiveness, and walking in Your word because You sacrificed and continue to sacrifice for me. I thank You, God, with every breath I have within me! You are magnificent, and I give my love to You again and again, every day!!!

In Jesus' Name,
Amen...

Love, "Nick Name"

Notes

Blessings and love…

I hope this book has brought you closer to our God!

We all face moments when we feel hopeless, yet prayer brings us back in line with the Father!

Many wishes for a prosperous and full life!

AMEN…

Love,
Faith